St. Francis and the Christmas Miracle

and other stories for children

by Fr. Chester Wrzaszczak

Resource Publications, Inc.
160 E. Virginia St. Suite 290
San Jose, CA 95112

Editorial Director: Kenneth Guentert
Production Editor: Scott Alkire
Book Design: Kevin Heney
Mechanical Layout: Geoff Rogers, Ron Niewald
Illustration Concepts: Charlotte Smalley

ISBN 0-89390-091-5
Library of Congress Catalog Card Number 86-062619
Printed and bound in the United States 5 4 3

ii

Table of Contents

To You Children

This book was written with LOVE. We had you in mind every word of the way. We were also thinking, as we authored this book, of the children of St. Anne Parish,[1] Portland, Oregon. They heard many, many stories from the mouths of my muppets — Freddie the Frog, Louie the Lamb, Manners the Monkey, and others — as they sat around me before the altar.

All the stories in this book are based in some way on incidents that happened to this author and to his illustrator,[2] Charlotte Smalley, during the dark Depression Days. We really experienced poverty — not having enough to eat at times; very little money; unable to pay our debts. We often wore heavily patched clothing and received few Christmas gifts. Our parents, both mom and dad, frequently worked long hard hours for a scant salary, especially because they were immigrants who did not speak English or have many skills.

But we kept the Faith.

Don't let those little numbers above different words you see from time to time distract you too much. They are

---

1. Your local, neigborhood church.
2. An artist who draws pictures in magazines, books, etc.

intended to increase your vocabulary[3] and give you a better and broader word-treasury. Just look up the corresponding number.

English is a beautiful language. Love it; learn it; use it properly. Read much. Jesus loved his native language, Hebrew.[4] He told marvelous, fascinating stories to children — as well as grown-ups. We wrote our stories in His spirit and love — and hopefully with His blessings.

Father Chester Wrzaszczak[5]
Pastor Emeritus,[6] St. Anne Parish
Portland, Oregon
St. Joseph Day, March 19, 1986

P.S. The pronunciation[7] guide is my own invention.

---

3. Word list.
4. Hee-brew
5. My last name is pronounced V-shah-sh-chock, but you can call me Father Chester.
6. A retired pastor still living in his parish.
7. Pro-nun-see-ay-shun, the proper way of saying a word.

To You Parents

You too were in our minds and hearts when we, the author and artist, Charlotte Smalley, wrote and illustrated these childhood recollections of the "Great Depression," and even before. We felt you belong to our family-circle of potential readers for two reasons:

First, many of you might want to relive your own childhood days and youthful encounters with Christmas with all its eager expectations. These tales may revive nostalgia, rekindle old fires, remind you of past sorrows as well as joys.

Secondly, we desire most ardently that, having read these stories for yourselves first, you might seat your children or grandchildren on the rug around you and read to them. Perhaps you might take your child or grandchild on your lap, or, when you tucked him or her into bed, and recount these memories to them. If your young hearers aren't ready for the book, tell the tales in your words. Improvise. Your author did — when recalling these same childhood tales.

As in our foreword to the children, so here too we refer to the love and story-telling prowess of the most inspiring story-teller that ever lived — the Son of God. His stories are immortal, ageless, because they deal with Eternal Life and Everlasting Love.

We, in our humble little way, just hope and pray our stories too will inspire and enrich all our readers.

The Rev. Chester Wrzaszczak

Acknowledgments

My deepest appreciations to Charlotte Smalley, who not only inspired the illustrations for ten children's tales, but also proposed basic plots, pointed to practical insights and presented valuable suggestions when most needed. We bounced ideas off each other for several years before launching this literary ship.

I am also deeply indebted to Sister Mary De Porres, CSSF, head of the Social Service Department, St. Francis Hospital, Milwaukee, Wisconsin. Despite her 12-14 hour day, she managed miraculously to type manuscripts sent to her almost weekly. Her grammatical aid was also invaluable. Sister Veronette, SSJ, one of Chicago's outstanding kindergarten and first-grade teachers, now at Our Lady of Good Counsel School in that city, gave us important information on the behavorial patterns of children in primary grades.

Patiently waiting for this work to appear, since they lived out some of the stories I've written, and encouraging me to publish, are my sisters: Frances Pfaff and Rose Baldridge, as well as my brother, Joseph Winters. Please forgive some of the fiction, dear ones!

Most of all, I thank Almighty God for making the final years of my extremely active — and exhausting — ministry of 42 years so rich, so rewarding, so fulfilling. In his mysterious, marvelous manner, He sent me to St. Anne Parish, Portland, Oregon, where I had the blessed, beatific privilege of being surrounded, especially at the Children's Masses, by so many hundreds of youngsters over a span of 12 unforgettable years. I felt so much like Jesus, the greatest story-teller that ever lived, as I tried to tell my stories. . .

Dedicated to Our Living and Deceased
Parents
Brothers and Sisters
Relatives and Religious
Fellow Parishioners
Friends — especially the young

St. Francis and the Christmas Miracle

This story took place in a small Midwestern town during "The Great Depression." Stephanie didn't like to call it that because, to her twelve year old mind, it seemed as though it meant "Sad Times." True, there were sad times but there were also happy times. So, instead of saying "The Great Depression," she spoke simply of "The Poor Times." Therefore, this story has a connection to an incident that happened to her during "The Poor Times."

It was Christmas Eve, the day before Christmas, 1931, in mid-morning. The temperature had dropped below zero, as is usual during a Minnesota winter. But by noon the thermometer rose and glorious snowflakes began falling. A little at first, then by the millions in an ever faster shower of white.

"A White Christmas!" shouted Stephanie, gazing joyfully out of the window. "We're going to have a White

3

Christmas!." Two sets of eyes joined hers, those of her older sister and her younger brother, Benji.[1] They gave voice to what they saw — and began dancing around the room, catching at last the holiday spirit.

It isn't easy to have the Christmas spirit, you see, when you're impoverished.[2] The Sadlers — Stephanie, Sigrid, Benji and their parents — were poverty-stricken.[3] The times were poor because there was no work for many people or little of it. That meant little or no money to buy presents. Sometimes there wasn't enough money to buy enough food to feed the family. The children began to feel blue, sensing that they might find nothing under their tree on Christmas Day.

As the soft flakes kept tumbling out of the gray, murky, wintry sky and became drifting snow, piling up by doorways and window ledges, the three children began to help their mother decorate the house. This was such fun! First, a scraggly but not too skinny a tree was brought in from the backyard, a left-over, given them by a tree dealer on the corner. Then came the pine boughs from the front yard, where stood tall, stately, evergreen trees. All worked happily — till it was time to sweep up the debris[4] and mop the floor. This the children disliked. The girls, being older and well taught by mother and the Sisters in school, offered up this less glamorous and boring work to Jesus. They hoped He would accept their offering and repay them tomorrow with Christmas presents. They forgot you shouldn't bargain with God but offer Him your sacrifice without asking for something in return.

---

1. Ben-gee. Short for Benjamin.
2. Poor.
3. Poor.
4. Pronounced "deh-bree." It means dirt, trash, etc.

But despite their prayers,, mother finally had to tell them sadly, " We have only that $20 bill in the sugar bowl that is kept on the top shelf of the pantry.[5] Remember, children, Daddy warned us not to touch it because he has to pay bills when he gets home early from work today." In those days many poor people kept small sums of money in a sugar-bowl for bills and emergencies. If any money was left over, it could be used for gifts at Christmas.

The girls broke into tears at this news. Benji would have cried the loudest but had taken the trash to the backyard, so was spared the sorrow. The two girls began begging mother to get presents first. The bills could wait, they sobbed. Now, mother knew that honest people pay their bills first. But, she felt so badly that she finally relented. "Just this once," she admonished her brood. "I'll try to explain this to your father when he gets home."

Sigrid, being the oldest, was entrusted with the twenty dollar bill. She was to get some groceries and three small bags of goodies, which would be their Christmas gifts for tomorrow. Overjoyed, Stephanie danced around the room as Sigrid raced for the clothes-closet for her hat, shawl, boots and coat. She disappeared into the snowy outdoors as Stephanie and Benji pressed their noses to the window pane and waited for her to return with those precious Christmas presents.

Sigrid dashed through the swirling snow towards town, just three blocks away, the $20 bill safely tucked inside her right hand glove. Unfortunately, she slipped on the ice and slid off the sidewalk. As she struggled to her feet, her glove was pulled partially off her right hand. She

5. Room between the kitchen and dining room for dishes, etc.

didn't notice the $20 bill blow away when she slipped and fell again.

It was a full half hour when she burst into the kitchen, tears streaming down her frozen, white face. She was covered with snow from head to foot, looking like a small, walking snowman. "Oh, mother, Oh, mother! I lost the money! The money slipped out of my glove when I fell!"

Consternation[6] struck the family. Grief was registered on every startled face. "What are we going to do? What are we to tell dad?" she moaned brokenly.

Stephanie, shocked though she was, breathed a short, fervent prayer to the Infant Jesus that the world was expecting the next day — and knew what must be done. Without a word to anyone, she reached into the closet, snatched her woolen tam and threadbare coat, but ignoring her needed boots, flew out of the house, tracing Sigrid's footsteps still faintly visible in the accumulating[7] snow.

It let up a little as Stephanie's eyes darted left and right while her feet brushed aside the snow-cover before her. Her lips moved in pleading prayer that somehow she might find that precious lost bill.

By now the lovely church of St. Francis, their parish church, began to loom before her. She whispered to herself, "I must go in and pray some more."

She turned into the driveway by the big oak tree as this was the shorter way to the side door of the church. She had taken but two short steps when she stopped suddenly, as if frozen stiff! There, up against that old

---

6. Panic, fearful excitement.
7. Piling up.

gnarled, oak tree, in a snowy hollow whipped up by the wind, like a green-feathered little bird huddled in its white nest, lay the crumpled $20 bill!

Stephanie could scarcely believe her eyes. "A miracle!" she shouted. "Thank you, Jesus! Thank you" she repeated fervently, snatching up the bill and clutching it tightly in her cold, cold hand. She had forgotten her gloves — but she had no frigid feelings — only the glow of gladness and joy!

It was less than an hour when Sigrid left the house and Stephanie returned. What cheering and embracing when Stephanie waved the highly-prized "green" before the family. Mother was red-eyed with weeping and forgot to scold Stephanie for leaving on such a sudden but most successful mission. She kept kissing Stephanie's snow-caked cheeks as Sigrid and Benji held her hands happily.

Then, amid the tumultous[8] celebration of this miracle on 32nd Street (where St. Francis church stood), loud knocking was heard on the door. Another seeming snowman strode through the door, flung open by Benji. "Daddy!" everyone screamed with joy. Brushing off the snow from his heavy overcoat and long stocking-cap and stamping his feet to clear his boots of slush, dad surveyed the family scene. Mother had mixed feelings. "Should I tell him? Should he be told a sad yet happy story about the lost-and-found money?" her maternal mind pondered.

Before she could utter a word, dad was reaching into the deep, roomy pockets of that outer, warm garment, chuckling and repeating "Ho-ho-ho," till out came one, two, three tiny sacks of candy and small toys. The children

8. Loud with shouts.

danced around him, hugging him around the waist. No, they wouldn't have to wait till tomorrow, since they hadn't tasted candy all Advent[9] and hadn't received a toy for an entire year, announced dad. Out of his jacket pocket, under his overcoat, appeared even a gift for his mother!

"The house is beautiful, mother," dad proclaimed, after taking off his boots and glancing with admiration at their decorated home. "I don't think I'll go out again into that snowstorm." I'll pay our bills, first thing, the day after Christmas." Mother stepped in front of dad, rather quickly, faced us and, without daddy seeing, put her little finger on her lips and shook her head slowly.

We understood. Dad would not be told. He was to be spared the story of a little disobedience on all our part.

Benji, however, spilled the beans! He missed the meaning of mother's secret message.

"Sigrid lost the $20 bill and Stephanie had to go out and find it!" blurted the boy.

Dismay and shame made everyone's face turn red. Mother's face was flushed too. She turned to dad sadly and apologized. "I'm sorry dad, but I felt bad about the children not having a happy Christmas. I sent Sigrid to buy a few things. She fell, lost the money but dear, dear Stephanie, managed to find it, miraculously!"

"It was a miracle, dad, really. I prayed to St. Francis and it was by St. Francis Church I found the money!" Stephanie exclaimed.

Dad was delighted.

He didn't scold us at all. He took mother in his arms. We closed around them like baby-bunnies around papa and mama rabbit. We cried for joy.

___

9. The four-week season before Christmas.

We had learned some lessons that Christmas — not to expect more than necessary, to be always open and honest with one another, especially to our parents — and to forgive,[9] as our father had forgiven us.

Oh yes, there was another lesson.

Miracles still happen.

10. To pardon.

The Windmill

Ciesiu[1] longed for an Erector Set. It was all he ever wanted. He dreamed of building a windmill, a fascinating windmill, that would whirl merrily in the wind. You see, Ciesiu one rainy day climbed to the attic of the house. The family called it "pustynia,"[2] a desert place, a place of quiet and peace for anyone to go when he or she needed.

The pustynia was indeed a peaceful spot. It had shelves of books, a bunk-bed, tables with magazines, newspapers, even an ice-box (no refrigerators yet) with refreshments: Kool-aid, ice-cream, candy bars. For those who wanted to pray, there was a small altar at one end of the room with a kneeler and a bench full of religious reading — the family Bible, especially. On this occasion,

1. "Cheh-shoe," Polish for "Little Chester" or "Little Ceslaus."
2. Pooh-stin-yah.

Ciesiu just wanted to read. A *National Geographic* magazine, with its familiar golden cover richly illustrated with persons and places in far-off lands, caught his eye, particularly the windmill on the cover. The magazine was featuring Holland as the main article. Ciesiu was activated as once. He read every word, even though his nine-year old mind didn't understand everything. "What a wonderful invention, the windmill!" he repeated to himself. The image of the whirling mechanical wonder was still vivid in his memory the next day when he passed a toy store in the shopping area. His eyes spied an Erector Set with a model bridge alongside it, constructed of Erector metallic pieces and many, many exciting parts. "Why, you can make a windmill with those same parts," he whispered with a low whistle of his pursed lips. "I have to get that Erector Set," he concluded, "I have to!"

But how?

Ciesiu's parents worked hard for a living. Money was scarce. It would be impossible to buy an Erector Set for the large sum of $5, which was the price-tag on Erector Sets in those days. He would have to do it the hard way, earn it, as the T.V. commercial today tells us!

People were kind but had to tell Ciesiu politely they had no odd jobs for him. Others sadly reported they just didn't have money to pay a boy to mow the lawns or rake up leaves. Neighbors phoned in suggestions but none proved promising. Ciesiu's parents soon learned of his efforts to raise funds for his beloved windmill. Their eyes filled with tears. They were proud at his determination, sad at his lack of success. But their eyes also took on a gleam and a glitter as they began making plans of their own. His older sisters, Frania[3] and Rozia[4], and a younger brother, Jozef[5], decided to pray with Ciesiu that all would have dreams come true at Christmas time.

Christmas was fast approaching. Snow was piling up high but boys and girls couldn't shovel the snow as there was much of it and, again, people just couldn't afford to pay others to do it, even if they were able. The snow at this time of year was soft and heavy, saturated with frozen moisture.

One morning Ciesiu served at the 6 a.m. Mass in his parish church. Usually older boys took the early Mass. Ciesiu was asked by Father Hester to substitute for a sick server. He agreed, as he knew this would please God and relieve Father Hester of looking for someone else. It was already getting late. Excited about serving at so early an hour, Ciesiu didn't sleep well, afraid he might not hear the alarm clock at 5:30 a.m. Because of this, he fell asleep at his desk later the next day, dreaming of his beloved windmill. Sister awakened him gently. She understood. She saw Ciesiu at the altar that morning. Sisters always attended early Mass in those days together with lay people on their way to or from work. However, she sent a note home to his mother, advising that the dear boy get more rest.

Ciesiu tried to explain to his mom his dream about the windmill and the Erector Set. Mother kissed his flushed cheeks and sent him up to the pustynia to rest and be quiet for a while. Ciesiu's father heard in the other room the conversation with a merry twinkle in his eyes. His plans for Ciesiu's dream were taking shape. People

3. Frah-nya, meaning "Little Frances."
4. Ruh-yah, meaning "Little Rose."
5. You-zef, meaning "Little Joe" or "Joey."

13

used to remark how Ciesiu's dad often had such a smiling look, even though he was poor.

Christmas Eve arrived at last and Ciesiu was selected to serve the Children's Mass at 6 p.m. He couldn't wait. Father Hester always brought his muppets, who explained to the children why the Christ Child was born on Christmas Day. The church would be full of excited children. They would gather around Father Hester before the altar and sit on the rug, filling all the aisles. One group of children, on the right, would be dressed as shepherds and wise men and kneel before Jesus, Joseph and Mary. Another group, on the left, would be the children's choir. Father called them "The King's Kids" because, as his muppets told the congregation, "Jesus is our King. We are his brothers and sisters; therefore, we are the King's Kids! Hurray!"

The muppets were always "Freddie the Frog," who did most of the talking, "Louis the Lamb" or "Manners the Monkey" and others. Father really did the talking, but the smaller children didn't notice this. St. Nicholas was always present — with Mrs. St. Nicholas. "Freddie the Frog" would explain that "Santa Claus" was really St. Nicholas. Even the sound of those two names almost tells you this. St. Nicholas was a good bishop who wore red, as all bishops, and had a peaked cap, oh, long ago, doing good, giving gifts to the poor for Jesus' sake. So he belongs; he really is part of this great gift-giving season, Christmas." The children would clap and the smaller ones would touch Father's hand or reach out to St. Nicholas. The Mass would begin. Children would also do the readings, delivering the "Glad Tidings," the "Good News" of Jesus' birth. After Mass, four children would stand at the four church doors and hand out wrapped chocolate bars and chocolate kisses. Everyone also got a balloon from St. Nicholas. One of the muppets would always remind everyone that Christmas Mass was a "Birthday Party" for Jesus, to celebrate His coming to us.

Elated, excited over the Children's Mass he served, Ciesiu started running home with the candy and balloon — but soon he slowed down. There wouldn't be any presents at home. Why hurry? Snowflakes began covering his stocking cap, then his sweatered shoulders and chest. "That's a present from Jesus," he thought to himself. "Snowflakes are beautiful." Once, under a microscope Sister showed the pupils how every single snowflake is different from the other — and all have fantastic forms. Some are star-shaped, others triangles, squares, rectangles. "How marvelous is God!" spoke the boy to himself.

Now Ciesiu was nearing home. To his surprise the house was all lit up. Usually only one light, in the living room, was on because the family was too poor to afford lots of lighting. The electric bill had to stay low enough for dad to pay it every month.

The family was at home. Dad would take them all to Mass the next day. When he opened the door sadly, suddenly the whole family shouted, "Surprise!" There, under the Christmas tree was the Erector Set! Ciesiu's face brightened at once, as if it had been plugged into a light socket by an invisible wire. He was overjoyed not only to see a gift for him but also presents for his sisters and brother. Mother and dad were smiling sweetly, happily. You see, they had often gone without lunch, just to save enough money to buy Christmas presents for all their children. Only later would Ciesiu notice that his beloved parents seldom bought new clothes for themselves, simply so that the family could survive in those poor times.

Amid shouts of laughter the children opened their

15

gifts. Ciesiu with trembling hands lifted the lid of the Erector Set. How shiny appeared the metallic parts and pieces! Now his dream would be realized! He would have his windmill at long last!

But, to his surprise and dismay, Ciesiu's dream began to crumble, as if it were a sand-castle on the beach with the sea rising around it, washing it away. Ciesiu discovered sadly that he was too young to understand the complicated instructions on how to put the set together to fashion a windmill. The set was actually designed for older boys.

His father noticed Ciesiu's perplexity. Ciesiu blurted out to him, "I guess Santa will have to take it back. I can't put so many parts and pieces together by myself." Dad replied, "Let's sit down and reason together," a favorite Bible quotation of his from Isaiah. "We will read the directions slowly and carefully." This was very generous of Ciesiu's dad since he couldn't read English too well. He had come from Poland and never attended school in America.

It was a charming scene, a peaceful picture of a family happy at home on Christmas Eve. Frania, Rozia and mom were admiring each other's presents; little Joseph was reading a fantastic fairy-tale book that was placed under the Christmas tree for him. Ciesiu and dad were kneeling near the Christmas Crib with the Erector Set parts strewn all around them. Perhaps the Baby Jesus loved what He saw. Perhaps He thought another gift would be appropriate for the occasion.

The gift?

Ciesiu's windmill put together, of course!

Yes, the directions began to make sense. The pieces managed to fit, just as when you work on a jigsaw puzzle. And no wonder Ciesiu couldn't construct the windmill.

16

The Erector Set was missing the whirling blades! Dad knew now what to do. He reached for the red cover of one of the now empty Christmas present boxes. With his pocket-knife he deftly cut out four red propellers or windmill flaps. Ciesiu was ecstatic. The whole family stopped to look and admire the holiday creation. All clapped their hands in appreciation at dad's cooperation — and God's blessings.

It was such fun!

For years afterward, Ciesiu and his family referred to this event as "The Year of the Windmill".

Aren't you glad?

Sonja's Magic Skates

Just one house from Sonja's house was the school. This was the first winter that the school yard boasted of a real ice-skating rink.[1] Sonja was both glad and glum.

Everyone, it seemed, was there. Everyone had skates, it seemed — except Sonja. She would run and slide on the ice, pretending she was on skates. How she dreamed of the day when she would be skimming in ecstasy around and around on the smooth surface of the school's ice-skating rink!

Finally, she found courage to ask her dear father for

---

1. Not to be confused with ring, which is also used in another athletic contest — the boxing ring.

a pair of those so long dreamed of and so eagerly desired skates. Dad heard her out patiently, as always, then said, "We'll see!" which usually meant "No." Her heart sank within her. "You can only dream so much while only sliding and not skating," Sonja sadly thought.

Christmas was coming. Store windows were filled with wonderful displays of delightful dreams. In one shop, which also sold sporting equipment, Sonja saw her dream skates. They were silver and white with laces up to the ankles. "Just super!" she whispered in awe, her eyes glued on the fascinating footwear for ice, while her nose pressed hard to the cold window pane of the store. "Perfect for me!" She had never seen anything, it seemed, so appealing to her in all her ten years of young life.

Sonja began to pray. She prayed to St. Nicholas, as Sister in school said he is the original, the real Santa Claus. St. Nicholas is said to bring children gifts in many parts of the world, especially Holland, on December 6th, though their parents did, of course; then the Christ Child on December 25th in many other countries and, finally, the Wise Men on January 6th in still other lands. Father Hester at the Children's Christmas Eve Mass, always at 6 p.m. (so the children could get home by 7:15 p.m.), calls this period between December 6th and January 6th, "The Gift-Giving Cycle." Jesus, in the center of this "cycle," inspired St. Nicholas to do good and to give gifts to the poor. Thus, because of Him the Wise Men also brought gifts. So, Sonja, who no longer believed in Santa, now knew that St. Nicholas was real and appealed to him in prayer. She also knew that you had to be good and do good to others. She decided that, since it was Advent,[2]

2. Different from Lent, which is the 40 day period before Easter.

that is, the four weeks before Christmas, she would help mom with some of the housework, like dusting. Her little brother, Bernie, needed to have his shoes polished; she would do it. In those days, people wore leather shoes, not sneakers or sandals; shoes needed polishing regularly.

Mother noticed Sonja's industrious endeavors. She asked curiously, "Why are you such an angel lately? You are a very good girl but you really are more helpful than usual." Mother's eyes were soft and hazel and full of love. Sonja explained about the skates and her prayers to St. Nicholas. Mother looked down kindly on her daughter. She stroked Sonja's glistening black hair, much like her father's, and replied wistfully, with sadness in her low, musical voice, "I appreciate your faithfulness — and your faith. But I don't think you should build up your hopes too high. We are rather poor and even St. Nicholas might miss our house this Christmas."

"Children used to find goodies in their wooden shoes in Holland on December 6th," remarked Sonja defensively. "True, child. I'll pray, too. However, remember, sometimes an answer to our prayers is 'No.'" With that, she kissed Sonja on the cheek, ran her hand fondly over her shoulder while Sonja wrapped her arms around her mother and sobbed.

In the final week before Christmas Sonja was tossing snowballs at the snowman she made with her friend, Sally, near the ice-skating rink. Soon one of her classmates, a new-comer, came by, Krisie by name. Sally whispered to Sonja, "She's not very bright. No one wants to be her friend. And I don't either!"

Sonja was aghast, startled that her companion would make such an unchristian remark. "I'm sorry, Sally," she sadly replied, "We must love everybody and not judge others."

Sally ran off in a huff, angry that her best friend preferred a girl who wasn't considered very bright. Sonja with a shy smile called out to the girl, "Let's pretend we're on silver skates, like Hans Brinker in our story book, and slide on the ice." Startled at the unexpected, warm invitation to a cold sport, the girl, too, smiled. Soon both were flying on the frozen man-made pond, pretending they were ice-queens, skating with the famous Hans of Holland of fairy-tale fame. Krisie, the new girl, was elated, excited, at the friendliness and friendship she found in Sonja, as well as in their thrilling twirling on the ice in make-believe, silver skates.

Their faces flushed with the exercise and the sharp, snappy, December cold and windy weather, the two made their way to Sonja's home, where Sonja's mother invited them to some fresh, hot, buttered popcorn. How the girls giggled and laughed. "Krisie isn't too bright, true," thought Sonja, "but she is sincere, open and willing to listen as well as to talk."

Suddenly Krisie said loudly, "Jeepers! Gee-whiz, I forgot! My dad was to pick me up at the school yard! I better phone him. What's your address here?" The call just caught her father as he was leaving. In fifteen minutes, as the girls watched out of the window, a car came slowly by and stopped at the house. Krisie waved a fast goodbye to Sonja and dashed out of the door into the waiting vehicle.

It was a sleek, shining, light blue limousine. "A limo!" breathed Sonja unbelievingly. "Her father drives an expensive, beautiful limo!"

When Christmas Eve finally came, Sonja's family was decorating the Christmas tree. Again, in those days, it was customary to bring in and decorate the tree on Christmas Eve and not take it down till the holidays were over. Mother found it necessary once more, with deep regret, to remind the children that St. Nicholas, the truly historical Santa Claus, would perhaps not put in his appearance, or at least, she lowered her voice to hide her emotions, "He might not bring what you want."

Sonja, nonetheless, dreamt that night that she was skimming over the ice, gliding smoothly on her Christmas present, the white and silver skates. There was an angelic smile on her face.

Meanwhile, with misgivings, Sonja's mother and dad were placing their children's presents under the tree that night. The gifts weren't much, but they came from their poor and loving hearts. "It's the thought that counts," people often say. "More than the gift; the gift to share even what may be small, inexpensive, insignificant, is the important thing."

What were the gifts under the tree?

There was a dress-making kit for Sonja; a model balsa-wood plane for Bernie; cold cream for mother; cologne[3] for dad; poor people's presents to each other standing in St. Nicholas' stead, in memory of the newly born baby of Bethlehem, Who Himself, though God, chose to be poor.

A knock on the door.

Sonja's parents looked at each other in surprise. "Who could that be?" dad wondered. "It's pretty late to be out tonight."

Mother unlocked the door, slid the safety chain off the slot, cautiously opened the door a crack. There stood, not Santa, but a man, yes: short, stout and jolly in his fine, costly over-coat with its rich thick fur collar. In his hands —

---

3. Co-lone, sweet-smelling after-shave lotion.

a large box, gay with Christmas wrappings.

"My name is Myra, Nick Myra; Krisie's dad. Krisie was here the other day. I want you to have this. Your Sonja was kind to my daughter — and so were you. The popcorn you made, well, she'll never forget how good you were to her."

Then he was gone.

Mother held the big box in her trembling hands, unbelieving, shaking her head.

Next morning the children found four other surprises under the tree; a gift certificate for Bernie (for an electric train); two gift certificates for mom and dad to be used at the large downtown department store; and, of course, for Sonja not a certificate — but guess what?

You guessed it!

Lovely white and silver skates!

Santa Claus is really St. Nicholas.

And, St. Nicholas is often none other than loving people, like your father, mother, grandparents, even strangers like Mr. Myra, who want to do good and be good — as was St. Nicholas.

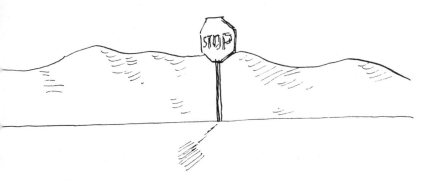

Christmas Pal

Little Alfred was sick in bed. It was necessary for him to be there some time. He had a bad ear infection. Mother decided to move his bed to the living room so he wouldn't be lonesome. He could look out of the big, bay[1] window and enjoy the street scenes and thus entertain himself. Mother had to busy herself with the usual household tasks.

Outside, it was bitter cold. Christmas was coming and the winter world was frozen fast with ice and covered with deep snow. Yet, despite the freezing weather, perhaps because of it and the approaching holidays, everybody was excited over the prospect of yuletide[2] presents and good cheer. Alfie, too, caught the fever, that is, he too began to feel the spirit of the season and to get excited.

You see, Alfred wanted so much to have a pet all his own. What he wanted most for this Christmas was a dog.

1. A picture window, that is, a larger window usually facing scenery or activity.
2. Another word for the Christmas season.

Dad, as usual, kept quiet. Mom told him it was best for him to wait as he was only five years old, not ready for the serious responsibility of taking care of an animal everyday. Besides, there were two older brothers and one sister in the family. They also wanted things for Christmas.

Now Alice, second oldest in the family, had a way with children. As often as she was free to do so, she would entertain Alfred by reading him stories and playing games: like monopoly, checkers, old maid, and so on. She even allowed him to stroke her long, brown hair which reached to her waist like a light chocolate-milk stream. Milk-chocolate was a favorite in the family.

It was now Christmas Eve, the day before that most joyous and gladsome of all holidays, when we celebrate the birthday of Jesus. Alfred grew restless at his continued confinement and unable to contain his excitement as he thought and yearned to have a "canine companion,"[3] as people often speak of a pet dog. Dad was expected home any minute. "What took him so long?" anxiously inquired Alfred. Perhaps it was the heavy snowstorm that dumped the "white stuff" even higher outside his bay window as the weather-man had announced on the radio. (There was no T.V. yet!).

Just then, there was a furious stamping of feet outside the door. Dad was scraping snow off his boots. At last the door-knob turned. In strode dad, holding tightly on a frayed rope a huge, shaggy — but a very happy-shepherd dog! The children screamed more in surprise than fear at this large animal, now barking furiously and wagging his tail as if it were a hairy propeller. Dad couldn't

---

3. Pronounced "Kay Nine," from the Latin word, meaning dog. During the war, dogs were called "K-9 corps" (pronounced "core" and meaning a group of soldiers).

hold or restrain him. The ragged rope broke; the dog bounded across the room — right into Alfred's arms! The bed became a soggy mess as man's best friend licked Alfred's face and hands and pawed his new master with his enormous, furry feet. By now all the children were clamoring for the pet's attention, surrounding the two in a human, happy circle, thanks to the thoughtfulness of their dad.

"My Christmas Pal!" shouted Alfred over and over again, not so much in jealousy that his brothers and sisters were petting his pal but to express his pleasure at the living Christmas present that finally fulfilled his desires and dreams.

Everybody was elated — except mother.

Mother was furious, aghast that another mouth had to be fed in their poor home and more work would result in having a dog running around the house and jumping with muddy feet into everyone's bed!

She began to cry.

"Arthur, Arthur! What have you done?" she despaired. Dad looked at her in silence. She wailed, "I told you — NO dog!"

Dad's face now creased itself in smiles. "I thought you would feel that way — but wait. Wait till I tell about this dog!" He chuckled as he continued, "He is a tramp dog. He's been riding the box-cars for weeks, like a hobo. He made friends with me and I just could not find it in my heart to abandon him over Christmas. Even an animal should be sheltered on Christmas Day. I'll take him back to the freight station and keep him there after the holidays."

"Never, never!" blurted out Alfred. "He's mine. I want him. He belongs here!"

"We'll see. We'll see." soothed mother, perplexed

and puzzled that her wishes about no dogs in the house were not honored.

The children, to placate[4] mother and appease[5] her, volunteered to bathe the "box-car hound," as mother called him under her breath.

What a jolly scene that was! The huge shepherd dog in the wash tub; his long, pink tongue hanging out; his pointed ears erect; his eyes laughing; his soiled coat covered with soap-suds; his body up to the neck in warm, cleansing water. The children splashed him. He splashed the children. Mother ran out of the room, throwing up her hands in despair at the sloppy floor. Dad sat back in his favorite chair and roared with laughter. "He's your pal now" daddy remarked.

And that's how the shepherd dog got his name, "Pal."

Pal became everybody's favorite. Everyone tried to teach him tricks, like sitting up, walking on his hind legs. Alfred wanted him to bow his head and place it between his front paws when grace[6] was said at table.

The biggest task, of course, for Pal was to learn toilet habits, to use the newspaper spread on the floor for him when no one was at home or to scratch on the door to be let out when a person was with him. This is called "Toilet Training," just like for a baby learning to walk and "to potty."

Needless to say, Alfred grew better by the day because of his canine companion, Pal. Even the doctor was surprised and mother was pleased. She would not relent, at least in her heart, and resolved the dog had to

---

4-5. These words mean almost the same, that is, to quiet someone or calm someone down.

6. To pray before eating is often described as "saying grace before meals."

go back to his box-cars at the freight depot[7] where dad worked.

One morning, the doctor decided that for Alfred bed-rest had to be joined to some outdoor exercise. "I believe," he told mother, "the boy should be dressed very warmly and allowed to go outside a little. The fresh air will do him a world of good."

Alfred clapped his hands. Dad, who was at home that morning since he had worked the "swingshift,"[8] spoke up. "I have just the thing for you. It was to be a Christmas present but the dog came first and I only finished last night what I intended to give you children on Christmas Day."

He disappeared down the cellar steps as surprise lit up Alfred's eyes. In a few minutes he reappeared, holding in his hands a home-made but very colorful sled with a little box affixed to it — for Alfred to sit in. A stout hemp rope was attached to the sled (nylon rope wasn't invented yet) as a harness for Pal.

Dad carried Alfred outside while mother carried the sled. Pal frisked about with the excitement of the moment, his tail wagging, eyes glowing and his bark deafening.

In the large yard the snow lay deep and undisturbed beyond the sidewalk. Pal could not understand his role so dad had to lead him by the collar and show him how to pull the sled. Mother held Alfred, bundled up in sweater, coat, shawl, stocking cap, mittens and ear-muffs, at her side, warning dad to be careful. Dad was encouraging Pal with the famous Eskimo cry to sled dogs, "Mush! Mush, you Husky!"

7. Pronounced "dee-poh." That's where railroad trains stop.
8. When you work from the late afternoon to late evening, for instance, from 4 to 10 p.m.

Pal was an intelligent dog, even though abandoned, perhaps lost. He caught on and understood he was to give Alfred rides in the yard.

Now, mother got into the act and supervised the fun when dad went into the house. She relented[9] a little but was still unsure the dog would stay.

That attitude changed dramatically the following morning. Dad had gone to work. Mother, struggling with the sled and Alfred both, lost hold of the sled near the gate.

The gate was half open. Someone forgot to shut it. The sled slid on the icy, slick sidewalk and shot out through the half-open gate — and headed for the street. In a flash, Alfred broke away from his mom and sped for the runaway snow vehicle,[10] now past the curb and bumping its way on the open street. With a cry, mother reached out for Alfred but lost her balance on the slippery walk and fell into a large snow-drift by the door.

Alfred never saw the car coming. His eyes were glued only on his precious sled.

But Pal saw his little master and bounded after him. The car was slipping and sliding as the driver stumped on his brake but couldn't stop it as it sped toward Alfred.

At the last moment Pal got there, clamped his large white teeth on Alfred's arm and pulled him to the side.

The car skidded past them, leaving the two safe and unharmed.

Pal was a hero.

Pal stayed.

Pal never had to be a hobo-dog riding the rails in a box-car again.

---

9. To relent means to give in, not to be set in your ways.
10. Anything that goes, like a car, truck, wagon, sled, etc.

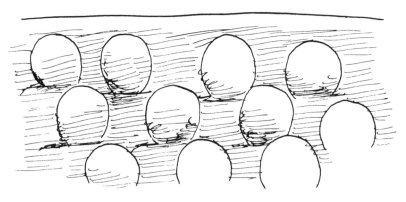

Mickey as the
Christmas Mouse

Mickey was six years old.

He was assigned to Mrs. Maher's class because he was an "underachiever."[1] This means that Mickey was not necessarily a slow learner but, because of his overly sheltered life at home, he had difficulty in coping with everyday life in school and out of school. This tore Mrs. Maher apart; that is, she felt very bad that the children sent to her were suffering from fear, shyness, loneliness, confusion. They were just not prepared to study, play, be friends with other children. They didn't know how; either there were no other children where they grew up or they

1. Ah-chee-ver.

could not be with boys and girls for some other reason.

Added to this problem was the fact that Mickey was part Indian and part black. Many people, especially white grown-ups, hated or would have nothing to do with someone who wasn't white like themselves. This is called racism.[2] It is wrong to hate people.

Mrs. Maher regarded Mickey as an adorable boy, a child of God, a lovely 6-year old with big, dark eyes; long, curly hair; slight build; a perfectly oval face; well proportioned nose; delicate hands; small feet.

It was most difficult for Mickey, whose real name was Michael (but his father called him Mick or Mickey before he deserted him and his mom) to realize he had to go to school. The very thought of being away from his beloved and loving mother to be among strangers — that is, among children he did not know — was very frightening to him.

So, on the first day of school, Mickey held his mother's hand so tightly that his and his mother's knuckles showed white. He dragged his heels, unwilling and afraid to enter the school building. Mother had to pull him up each stair.

Then, when the monitor came to welcome Mickey to class, even though the monitor was just an older boy assigned to help Mrs. Maher, Mickey broke away from his mother's grasp, bolted under the nearest desk and stayed there, refusing to come up.

Mrs. Maher and the monitor asked mother not to worry but to leave Mickey and go home. Reluctantly and unsure of the outcome, mother left. All morning long (classes lasted only a half day) Mickey huddled under the

2. Ray-sizz-zym.

desk. Mrs. Maher talked to the children — and to Mickey — without mentioning that he was out of sight. The other children seemed to understand and said nothing. No one laughed or pointed a finger.

This went on for three months! Every morning Mickey ran for the same desk and dived under it. Mother would leave and return at noon to escort him home. "Patience," said the teacher, "it's our only hope." She noticed how longingly Mickey looked at the children, especially when they sat in a circle on mats on the floor around Mrs. Maher. Every child, he noticed, had his and her own little gaily colored rug to sit on. And, oh those gorgeous pictures on the walls: animals, farms, fields, hills. How he wished he could join in the fun and be close to all the activities! Yet he could not. He just peered out from under the desk as if he were a small, frightened rabbit in a cage. He even looked like a scared bunny when Mrs. Maher tried to feed him. He was afraid to touch the food even though it was in the form of cookies, cake, candy. He ate all that his mom gave him at home but he just couldn't reach out to take what was offered him in school.

Now, just after Thanksgiving, which had been such a festive time, the first graders began making plans for Christmas. Mrs. Maher read to them the famous poem, "Twas the Night Before Christmas." They were delighted! They decided with the teacher's help, of course, to dramatize[3] the poem. Each child would act out one part of the poem at the schools's Christmas Pageant.[4] Mickey was all eyes and ears. Without realizing it, while thinking how wonderful it would feel to be in the Christmas play,

3. Put into the form of a stage-play.
4. Peh-gent. A colorful play or celebration.

Mickey began to slide out from under his prison-desk. Slowly, uncoiling his cramped legs, as if a crab "crashing its pad,"[5] he was leaving his place of confinement. Mrs. Maher pretended not to see.

Mickey crawled away from that desk, closer, closer to the circle of children. There were two empty chairs very near to him. He slipped silently into one. The boy near him looked, smiled and said nothing, as if that's where Mickey belonged. Mrs. Maher had asked the children never to show surprise at anything Mickey might do, especially if he decided to join the class. Secretly, they were overjoyed that Mickey was now part of their daily life.

Then Mickey spoke.

Mickey uttered his first words in school!

Mickey said, his voice high with excitement, "Can I take the part of the 'Christmas Mouse'?" Instinctively and spontaneously the children began to clap. Mrs. Maher's eyes filled with tears of joy. Lovingly, with a very misty look, Mrs. Maher replied in her usual, gentle tone, "Why certainly, Mickey. That would be very nice. I think you'll make a nice 'Christmas Mouse.' "

Mickey never went back into hiding under the desk. Instead, he sat in it, as the children, as if he had always sat there. He almost had the air of a conqueror,[6] a king, sitting on his throne. The children cheered inside themselves.

As the plans began taking form in the busy, bustling days that followed, doubts began to surface in Mrs. Maher's mind about Mickey's ability to perform in public. He still was shy at times. He kept missing his cue,

5. Escaping.
6. One who won.

forgetting when it was his turn to come out from behind the curtain. Most of all, he could not understand what Mrs. Maher meant when she said all children had to get their own costumes for the play. Finally, she decided to pin a note to Mickey's shirt for his mother to read. However, as she looked into Mickey's deep, dark eyes, on impulse she thrust the note into his small hand, smiled her ever sweet smile and stated simply, "Mickey, take this note home to your mother. It tells her about your costume. You won't lose it, will you? I trust you to take it to her yourself, now that you go home without her." She pressed the folded paper into his grasp, patted him on the shoulder. Proud and pleased that teacher trusted him to deliver an important message, Mickey sped homeward without stopping. He lived only a block and a half from school.

Mother embraced her son warmly when he explained how Mrs. Maher had entrusted him to deliver the request personally to her. She was so satisfied that her dear slow achiever of a son was making such steady progress.

Excitement mounted as Christmas drew even closer for the first graders. Mickey was responding better and better to direction during the daily rehearsal. As yet, mother hadn't made his mouse-suit. Mrs. Maher thought of sending another note to Mickey's mom but concluded the poor mother was over-worked or had difficulty in sewing the costume. Some mothers can't sew as well as others. Sewing is a talent which must be developed with practice, done many times over.

On December 23rd, which was a Thursday, the children helped Mrs. Maher decorate their classroom and put up the Christmas tree. Such chatter and chit-chat, like a squadron of squirrels surrounding a nut-laden oak!

Mickey, who had aided his mother in decorating the house and tree since he was four, was able to help.
Mrs. Maher's eyes sparkled at the sight of the children's enthusiasm and united effort.

Dress rehearsal was to follow. Everyone had his and her costume. At the last minute Mickey's mother appeared at the door. She confided to Mrs. Maher that she finally decided to use an old bedsheet for Mickey's mouse outfit. "I wanted to save money for Mickey's Christmas present and couldn't afford to buy gray cloth. I dyed a sheet a mousey gray!" The teacher was tickled to see how expertly mother had contrived the costume.

The rehearsal however, did not go well. Perhaps the children were taken up too much with their new stage-clothes. Some tripped over their long gowns. One little girl ripped open a seam, another spilled orange pop over herself. Had not Mrs. Maher experienced similar scenes in her many years of teaching, she might have despaired at the outcome of tomorrow's performance.

Came at last Friday, December 24th, the last day of school before the Christmas holidays. The auditorium overflowed with families of the school children. An air of joyous expectation filled the large hall. The rich aroma of popcorn and hot chocolate permeated the building. Walls, ceilings, even some floors bore decorative designs of the season: snowflakes; Santa; star-lit skies against satine, black backgrounds; gay green and radiant red, the traditional colors, everywhere.

Now the lights began to dim. Last-minute loiterers[7] and late-comers scrambled for their seats. The Christmas Pageant was about to begin.

---

7. People just standing around.

40

The curtain began to open, slowly, then faster.

There was the stage with the winter-set, a back-drop of snow-covered homes nestled in a long-ago hamlet[8] amid a silent night, the night before Christmas. One after another the actors of Grade One appeared, speaking their piece, acting out their role, reciting those memorable magic lines.

All was progressing smoothly, till . . .

You guessed it — no Mouse.

Where was the Christmas Mouse? Where was Mickey in his mouse-costume? The low murmur of voices of people in the audience hushed still.

Mrs. Maher was about to have her heart attack — as Mickey was nowhere to be seen!

Then, suddenly out he swept from the wings and on to the stage. He faced the audience boldly, wiggled his whiskers hilariously, coyly skipped about the stage just like a real, live mouse! The people cheered, clapped, roared with laughter at the superb performance.

"Mickey Mouse!" everybody shouted with glee and with another round of applause.

Mickey was the hit of the evening, the star performer. He "stole the show," as people say of a star.

"What a present the Christ Child gave me!" Mrs. Maher exclaimed in rapture[9] afterwards, kissing and congratulating him. "The Baby Jesus gave me this dear boy to teach and train. My Christmas is complete; my teaching career has reached its highest peak!" she exulted.[10]

What about Mickey's lines? What words did Mickey

---

8. Small village.
9. In great happiness.
10. Said with triumph, as a winner.

say on the stage on that never-to-be-forgotten night?

What would you expect from a shy boy, playing the part of a mouse?

"EEEK," of course!

44

Didi's Dimples

Didi[1] first saw her at the shopping center.

It was early December. Didi's mom had taken Didi to the downtown department store when school was out that day because of the teachers' workshop.[2]

Didi accidentally strayed into the toy section of the huge store while her mother was busy admiring some dainty dresses for Didi's two younger sisters. Everywhere there were playthings for children — and even for grown-ups. They were heaped high on counters, in display cases, on racks, for Christmas shoppers to see.

Nothing, really, interested Didi except some jig-saw puzzles, which she loved to put together. Then her eye caught sight of the doll, the most adorable little doll she

1. Pronounced "Dee-dee."
2. Meeting of people to help improve their skills.

had ever seen. She was neat; a doll that looked like a lovely young lady, though doll-size. She was a dream with ebony-black hair cut in the latest style; long, curling, dark eye-lashes; a delightful dimple in each cheek; an exquisitely shaped chin; high cheek bones; a delicate set of tiny ears from which dangled imitation[3] pearl pendants[4]; her clothes representing the most modern fashion on the market. Her petit[5] feet were encased in patent leather pumps. In those days patent leather shoes were the "rage."[6]

But, because of those delightful, little indentations in the doll's cheeks, which reminded her of her own, there and then Didi decided to name the doll, "Dimples." Didi's own parents were delighted, when Didi was born, to see her dimples. The other two children had dimples in their knees or elbows only.

Slowly, with awe and baited breath, Didi stretched out her hand, Tenderly, gently, she touched "Dimples," first her hands, then her face and hair. "Why, she's a perfect princess!" whispered Didi in admiration. That did it. "She was 'sold' on the doll," as her mother would tell her dad later. She fell in love with her the moment she saw her."

"I fell in love with you, dear," dad said gallantly[7], "when I first saw you, mostly because of your dimples." Mother blushed but was pleased at dad's first recollection[8] of her. Both parents understood, then, how Didi felt.

---

3. Make-believe.
4. Earrings.
5. Pet-teet, French for "tiny."
6. Meaning very popular, "tops," "the most."
7. Like a gentleman.
8. Memory, reminder.

However, many people in that era,[9] some of whom you met in the other stories in this book, were too poor to buy even inexpensive playthings for their children. Some boys and girls were fortunate if they received candy for Christmas — or any other time of the year.

"How can I get that doll?" Didi pondered and debated[10] with herself.

Mother had to go "downtown" again. Didi asked to accompany[11] her. Mother suspected the reason. She remembered how Didi lovingly touched the doll when she found Didi in the toy department. "I mustn't allow her to go looking for that attractive doll" mother reminded herself.

But to Didi's horror, as she broke away from her mom's handhold, her precious dream-doll was gone!

"Where's Dimples?" she cried. "They sold my doll!" she sobbed loudly as tears rained down her face, flushed with the sudden, sad surprise of discovering her beloved gone. "Christmas is only eleven days away. I'll never see or have Dimples, never!" she moaned listlessly.

Mother wiped away Didi's tears with her lavender-scented[12] hankerchief and comforted her daughter, speaking softly. "Some nice girl will give Dimples a good home and lots of love, I'm sure, Didi. Offer your sorrow to Jesus. Your acceptance of not getting what you wanted right away will be your Christmas present to Jesus."

Didi returned home, solemn,[13] silent, somewhat subdued. Mother, too, was silent and sad. She made some hot chocolate for both of them. They sat quietly,

9. Time-period.
10. Argued.
11. Go along with.
12. Smelling of lavender, a purple, fragrant flower or plant.
13. Serious.

sipping their delicious dairy drink. Mother always added milk to bring out the fine flavor of chocolate. Both reflected[14] on their afternoon experience.

"I know that some fortunate, deserving, young miss will get that lovely doll" mother remarked cautiously. Didi almost choked as she attempted an answer that never came. She excused herself and quickly dashed outdoors. She didn't want mom to see her in tears again. She was back soon. It was cold outside and Didi wanted to help mother with the laundry. To make a few dollars more, so as to feed the family, Didi's mother "took in washing," that is, she washed and ironed other people's clothes. Didi always folded the clothes when mother took them off the clothes-line. Dryers for home use weren't yet invented. Often, too, Didi was allowed to press some of the smaller things, like hankies, hand-towels and napkins. With the Christmas season fast approaching, more people were sending in their laundry. Didi was kept busy. This helped keep her mind off her beloved doll. However, every time she sorted baby clothes to fold and iron, her eyes would fill with tears. Baby things resemble a doll's wardrobe.[15]

Finally, it was Christmas Eve, the day before Christ's birthday. Didi went carolling early afternoon with her classmates. They always sang for the "senior citizens" (as elderly folk are often called) at several convalescent[16] homes. At these nursing homes[17] or facilities[18], as they're also called, the patients, mostly grandmothers and grandfathers who no longer had anyone who could care

14. To be in deep thought.
15. Collection of clothes.
16. Homes for people recovering from illness, also homes for older people who need special care.
17. Same as number 16 above.
18. Places of service to people, as hospitals, schools, etc.

for them properly, waited for the carollers. They loved the many youngsters who came to sing to them at this joyful part of the year. The fourth-through-eighth graders often got kissed, hugged and embraced by these aged[19] shut-ins. They would stroke the children's faces, admiring their complexion:[20] the pink, young, smooth soft skin and the sparkle of youthful eyes. "How I wish I were your age" some would state wistfully. Others sighed, "I have grandchildren who look like you"; or, "To think I used to be as you are now!" The singers also brought small presents for those senior-citizens: chocolate "kisses" (resembling lttle silver bells), handkerchiefs, socks. The children felt so good to be loved and needed. They also realized with wonder that someday they might be in such homes themselves.

By 4 p.m., when everything was over, the carollers would head for their homes, excited, elated[21] at making bright lonely, old hearts on Christmas Eve — and impatient to start preparing for their own Christmas. Many families in by-gone times shared in the fun of decorating the Christmas tree on Christmas Eve. They gather today to share in the family dinner on Christmas day itself.

Silently the snow was falling, filling the already darkening day with the festive[22] atmosphere[23] and spirit we associate[24] with Jesus' Birth at the beginning of winter.

Home at last, Didi helped decorate their home. She was delighted at the perfect symmetry[25] of their little

---

19. In this case, the word has 2 syllables (sill-lah-bulls), as "A-jed."
20. Color and appearance of face.
21. Filled with joy or pride.
22. Holiday-like.
23. Air.
24. Connect with, join to, etc.
25. Fine form, appealing shape.

Christmas tree. It was full — as befits the pine and spruce and cedar of Yuletide.[26]

Bedtime came at 8 p.m. for her smaller sisters; for Didi it arrived at 9 p.m. She did the dishes for mom and drowsily, absent-mindedly almost, wiped them before stumbling to her own bed. She murmured a "quickie" prayer and was fast asleep.

There never was too much excitement on their Christmas mornings. The gifts were usually small, inexpensive, almost always some candy, gum, a useful article of clothing, like a blouse. Once, there were popcorn balls and balloons — but nothing else.

Someone shouted, "We all have the same thing!" True enough. Didi poked her face out of the bedroom door. There were three identical boxes under the Christmas tree — one for each girl. Didi had no brothers. Dad and mother were there, holding each other at the waist, not caring that they didn't recieve any gifts. Their wreathed[27] smiles and sparkling eyes told a story of love. As long as the children were happy, healthy and holy, that was Christmas joy enough for them.

Didi's sisters ripped open their boxes. Each held a doll; the dolls were identical twins.

Didi's box also contained a doll.

The doll was — Dimples!

Didi was dumb-founded.[28]

Dad explained. "I suggested to mother that she buy Dimples on a lay-away plan." Mother broke in, "We paid a dollar a week for three weeks. We had three more payments to make, as I told Mrs. Winters, our nice next-

---

26. Christmas time.
27. Two syllables, wree-thed, that is like a wreath, entwined flowers.
28. Struck dumb, unable to speak.

door neighbor. Mrs. Winters noticed how you helped me with the laundry, especially how you delivered the wash on your sled the day the snow was so crisp and crunchy. Remember?"

"It was fun," Didi dismissed the recollected[29] scene with a wave of the hand, clutching Dimples tightly in the other.

The parents began to add further details of the story, the sweet, strange circumstances[30] that made the Christmas surprise possible.

"Mrs. Winters happened to visit her spinster[31] sister, who lives in one of those convalescent homes, where your group carols every year. This sister was so impressed at what she heard that she wrote out a check at once."

"To pay for your doll, Didi, and for the twin dolls," mother and dad finished triumphantly, in unison.[32]

Didi just shook her head unbelievingly as her sisters played with their presents.

"Let's go to church now" advised dad, "to thank the Baby Jesus for the love He showed us."

The family was happily humming "Adeste Fideles"[33] as the door closed upon their Christmas tree and the snow creaked under their feet.

At church Jesus was awaiting them.

---

29. Remembered, recalled to mind.
30. Events.
31. Unmarried, single.
32. Together, at the same time.
33. Ah-dest-tay Fee-day-less," a popular Latin hymn. These first two words mean, "O Come All You Faithful."

A Bicycle for Babe

It was a chilly, rainy day.

It was typical of Oregon, that is to say, in Oregon rain falls all winter long instead of snow, most of the time.

Babe wasn't thinking of snow.

She was thinking of what she saw Saturday in the store — a shiny, new bicycle. She wanted it so badly, so desperately, but she knew it was out of the question since it cost so much. Even now, her pretty mouth was puckered with pain at the thought that a bicycle wouldn't be hers for Christmas.

Christmas wasn't too far away. You wouldn't think so, if your were there, because as we said before, it rains in Oregon often, even on Christmas Day itself. Children, however, dream of Christmas presents the world over, whether there is snow on the ground or not.

Babe had joined the Girl Scouts when she had her 12th birthday. That's when the idea of riding a bike entered her mind. The Scout Troop had planned a Bike-Hike just before Babe was initiated[1] a scout. Now, everyone was excited and elated over this first event, due during the Christmas holidays.

How pert and pretty Babe appeared in her neat scouting-uniform! Her blonde hair was swept up in a darling top-knot and the glow of her peaches-and-cream complexion clearly indicated she was very proud and

---

1. Became a member.

pleased to be a member of an international organization, as is the scouting movement. Her sad brown eyes, however, and wrinkled brow told you something was wrong. She was unhappy. She wouldn't be able to participate in the mid-winter hike and take part in the fun along the biking path in one of Oregon's innumerable forests.

Babe's brother, Billy, two years younger than she was, or as mother put it, "two years her junior," had borrowed an old, rusty bike from a friend. He taught Babe one evening to ride, rickety[2] though the bike was.

It wobbled[3] because of its loose wheels. She screamed when he let go once but she quickly steadied herself and surprisingly maintained her balance. Her confidence was almost destroyed a half hour later, when she made a sudden turn and was thrown to the ground, where there was much gravel.[4] Gravel is very dangerous to bikers as is ice, of course. She skinned her knee, scratched her arm and felt foolish lying there with legs and arms entangled in the two-wheeled machine, for that's what the word "bicycle" means, a machine with two wheels. Well, Billy helped her up and gave her instructions how to make turns properly.

The bike needed repairs — so did Babe. Mother did not scold the children but spread ointment on her daughter's wounds after Babe washed off the grease and grit.[5] A large band-aid on the knee reminded them of a tire patch on their old Ford. They all laughed, even though it hurt Babe to realize that a bicycle of her own was

2. Shaky.
3. Moved unsteadily.
4. Loose stones and pebbles.
5. Sand and dirt particles.

still far from reality, only a dream, a deep desire.

After the old bicycle was mended, as well as babe's bumps and bruises, Billy showed Babe how to pump uphill and coast down, how to apply the brake gradually instead of at once — except in case of emergency. Traffic signals had to be learned and signaling amid moving vehicles[6] — to let motorists know whether you're going to turn right or left. A friendly city-policeman appeared at a Scout Meeting one night and explained these same rules to the girls. Babe often raised her hand when the patrolman asked questions. He praised her for the right answers and was sorry to learn that she was the only one there without a bicycle.

Returning home after the meeting, Babe couldn't help reflect on how time was flying. She reviewed in her mind the past summer. It had been filled with work, hard work, in their big, back yard. Dad had been ill and her older brother Bob, who did most of the yard work every summer, was working on Uncle Albert's farm in Iowa. Her dad needed her "muscle," as he described it, and she was proud he had confidence in her strength and ability to help out the family when needed. The grass had been invaded by dandelions and weeds were ruling everywhere. Dad wanted the dandelions to be dug up. For this he gave her his own sturdy pocket-knife, which he used for everything, from whittling wood to opening root-beer cans for the children (Pull-tabs on cans weren't invented yet). The weeds had to be pulled up by hand. All this required muscle but it also blistered Babe's hands and gave her an aching back. Yet, the fresh air, the warm sunshine, the exercise that she got from working made

6. Any car, truck, bus, etc.

Babe brown as bark with a healthy tan and her young body became more supple[7] and stronger each day. "Helping your parents and others, even when it's not easy, is good for body and soul" Father Hester, their parish priest, told the children in church one Sunday. He had the children sit around him, as he always did when he had "The Children's Mass" at St. Anne's. Through popular "Manners the Monkey" and "Freddy the Frog," Father's favorite two muppets, the youngsters were encouraged to be of service to "their fellow-men" by helping with lawn work, like mowing grass, pulling weeds, running errands, picking up and saving newspapers for recycling.[8] The next day Babe uncovered an old silver dollar, when digging up more dandelions. She felt it was some sort of a small reward for helping. She gave it to dad for his birthday.

"Now it's almost Christmas," sighed Babe. All the hints she dropped off wanting a bike seemed to go unnoticed. Everybody at home was busy with holiday preparations. They had little time for a girl whose dreams were too expensive and whose wants were too costly for them.

On Christmas Eve, December 24th, when all the world, it seems, is aglow with the glory of the Day to come, December 25th, Babe's family gathered to decorate the house and the Christmas tree. Dad and mom were cheerful, the children chattering like magpies in a garden laden with fruits and flowers — except Babe. She was silent, listless, sad. No chance to get that beloved bike.

---

7. Flexible, bending and twisting easily.

8. Using over again. Old newspapers can be made into new paper, roofing materials, etc. It's valuable.

Dad, she mused,[9] was working only part-time, as he never shook off his illness from last summer, and bills were piling high. The family was really struggling "to make ends meet," as mother expressed it. When the last glittering silver pieces of tinsel had been gingerly looped over the tree's branches and the glowing Christmas Star set atop the tree in triumph, the family picked up after itself, tidied up the room and quickly, quietly went to bed.

Babe tossed and turned that night, dreaming that her Scout Troop was departing on the Bike-Hike without her. She saw herself waving goodbye to her friends on their beautiful bicycles while she was left behind. She watched them disappear into the forest, deeper and deeper. . . Babe dozed off and fell into a fitful[10] sleep.

Suddenly, it was morning, December 25, Christmas day. "Wake up! Wake up!" the children were shouting to each other from their bedrooms, even though everybody was already up. They found mother and dad by the tree in their new dressing gowns, sipping coffee. Hot chocolate was brewing on the stove, awaiting the arrival of the children.

As her brothers and sisters rushed for their presents under the tree, Babe brought up the rear,[11] walking wearily, as if she had little sleep.

Then she spied IT!

She saw back of the tree, with its handlebars barely visible — HER BICYCLE!

She rubbed her eyes. Was this a dream, different from the other in which she was the only one not owning a bicycle?

9. Thought deeply about.
10. Uneasy, restless.
11. Was last.

In a flash, she was pushing aside the tinselled branches with their gay, gorgeous but very fragile tree-trinkets. One fell and shattered like an egg-shell. Tinsel fluttered to the floor.

But Babe was there, unbelieving, unable, as yet, to cry out.

Was it hers?

In big, bold lettering on the bicycle's cross-bar, in full view, was her name: B A B E.

"We wanna ride! Will you give us a ride, Babe?" was all she heard from all sides.

She looked up at dad.

He came, with mother at his side, smiling happily.

"We never forgot how hard you worked all summer. You earned that bicycle. We couldn't afford it, no way. We prayed. Our prayers were heard."

Astounded, Babe and the children, for the first time, heard the story.

"Remember that old silver dollar you dug up?" Dad asked.

"By the tulip tree!" exclaimed Babe. "Entangled in the roots."

"The one you gave me for my birthday," reminded her dad. "Well, I examined it carefully after cleaning off some cement at the bottom, where the date was engraved.[12] The date was 1879. I took it to a coin collector."

"It was worth $286.50!" mother interrupted. "Enough for all our presents — AND YOUR BICYCLE, BABE!"

There was silence.

---

12. Printed.

Then someone began to sing.

You would expect a traditional[13] Christmas carol.

It was a song the family heard once at a Prayer Meeting. Soon all were singing "Thank You, Jesus. Thank You."

13. Old-time, commonly used.

Florek's First
Christmas in America

Florek[1] was a Polish immigrant.[2] He was only five years old. This country seemed very strange to him, indeed. People spoke a different language. Everyone had so many things to eat and wear and play with, unlike his country, where people had so little.

Florek arrived with his mother, Mihalina.[3] They came to live with his grandmother, Godyslawa.[4] His "Tatus"[5] had to stay in Poland until they were situated, that is settled, and were able to find work for him. The job would have to be the kind an American would not need or could not do.

How Florek missed his father! He had no one to talk

1. Floor-rek.
2. A person who comes from another country to stay for good.
3. Mee-ha-lee-nah.
4. Goh-dyh-suave-vah.
5. Tah-toosh, meaning "dear daddy."

to except his mamusia[6] and babcia.[7] He could talk to his dad all the time in Poland. It was terrible to be so alone. Much as he loved his mom and dear, kind grandma, Florek longed to have friends to play with and discuss things, such as American customs,[8] toys, school, games.

One day, close to Christmas, Florek's father phoned from Poland. When the boy heard his father's voice, he shrieked with delight. His words tumbled out of his mouth like a waterfall. His father was happy too to hear his son, whom he also missed very much. Before he hung up, Florek's father promised him something special for Christmas. The boy wanted only one thing for Christmas — his Tatus. The only thing that Tatus could say was "We'll see." This, at least, spelled hope, since his dad did not say "No."

A week later a special delivery package arrived. It was addressed to Florek. Grandmother was busy outside and mother had gone downtown, job-hunting for her husband. Florek tore open the wrappings eagerly but was careful not to damage the many, colorful, Polish stamps. Grandma collected stamps in her large album she had kept for years. In the box, carefully folded, was a complete Polish costume — his size! Florek danced up and down, holding the red and white native suit against his body, admiring it in the full-length mirror in the hallway.

Grandma heard the boyish shouts. She burst into the house, alarmed. When she saw Florek standing there holding the gorgeous, gay boy's outfit from Poland, she broke into a lovely smile. Tears splashed down her cheeks as she remembered the native Polish dress she wore as a

6. Ma-moo-shah, meaning "dear mom."
7. Bob-chah, meaning "granny."
8. Ways of doing things, manners.

girl long ago. She was also over-joyed to see her grandson so happy, for a change.

Yet, she was very disappointed with Florek. "The package was to be a surprise" she scolded him. "It's your Christmas present. Christmas is four days away."

Florek's face flushed. He was crushed for two reasons. First, he had spoiled his Christmas surprise. Secondly, worse, his dad was not coming. That would have been the real Christmas surprise., his dad's arrival for the holidays. He began to sob. Grandmother Godyslawa gathered him into her warm, wide bosom[9], kissed away his tears while her own glistened in her gentle eyes. "There, there, now" she soothed him in her lilting, Polish language. "Put away your costume and wash up for dinner."

When his mother returned, Florek proudly displayed his present to her, apologizing that he had opened it before Christmas. Mother understood. After all, the box with the suit had the name of Florek on it. The costume was then put away into the dresser drawer for friends to see on December 25th, Jesus' Birthday.

That night Florek prayed that his "Tatus" would phone again on Christmas Eve. He wanted so much to thank him for his gift, even though he had seen it before time. Snow was already falling outside in the still darkness when Florek finished his prayers and was tucked snuggly into bed by those two lovely ladies who loved him so much, his beloved mamusia and babcia.

When Florek awoke, the world outside his window was dazzling white with a thick blanket of snow. For the next three days it snowed more, so that by Christmas Eve

---

9. Breast.

America appeared to Florek to be just like he saw pictures of it in his mother's old geography book back in Poland. The boy was allowed to bring in the Christmas tree which was almost his own size. Grandmother wanted it o be tall enough for Florek to decorate by himself. It was his first Christmas tree in the "New World," as she called the United States. He felt so grown up, putting the tinsel on the boughs of the tree, attaching electric light bulbs to the branches. His hands trembled and fumbled much, both because they were little and because his excitement was so great. His eyes grew wide at the sight of the tree-ornaments. Nothing like this did he ever see in Poland — beautiful, bespangled[10] balls of delicate, thin glass; pretty diamond-shaped plastic pictures with various winter scenes painted on them; silk streamers of crimson and scarlet. "I've never seen so many shades of red" he told his grandmother with hushed voice. "Neither have I" his mother whispered back. Her eyes, too, widened, at the variety and beauty of the Christmas decorations.

Florek had to take his nap by late afternoon. While he dozed, the two women festooned[11] the house with holiday garlands of red and green. Then it was time for all three to attend the Children's Christmas Eve Mass. Father Hester, pastor of St. Anne's, stood at the church doors greeting everyone. Florek hugged him when the priest wished him Merry Christmas in Polish, as did his mom and grandmother. The church was packed with people, mostly children. "Look, mom!" he gasped, "They have a living, real Christmas Crib!" True. In the center aisle in front of the altar stood a girl and a boy dressed as Mary and Joseph. Other boys and girls were in the costumes of

10. Having stars.
11. Strung out.

shepherds and wise men. A real live baby, a brother of the girl dressed as Mary, was Jesus! "I should have worn my costume," thought Florek, "and taken my place by Jesus, too. My Polish costume used to be worn by Polish shepherds!"

The Holy Sacrifice of the Mass, or "The Liturgy,"[12] as Father Hester called it, wasn't long. Father Hester and his muppets spoke first. "Louis the Lamb" told the children sitting around Father and the Living Nativity Scene (that is, the Live Crib) how the shepherds were told by angels about Jesus being born in a stable in Bethlehem. He told how proud he was to be a lamb because Jesus said He Himself was the "Lamb of God!"

With his balloon and "silver bell" chocolate kisses, Florek went home happy. Only one thing made him sad — his tatus was so far away!

When the family got within a block of their home, grandmother, nodding to Florek, said, "You'll find another present under the Christmas Tree besides your Polish costume. Why don't you race your mother to the house?"

Mother and son flew across the frozen snow, slipping and sliding but staying on their feet, laughing and shouting, leaving grandma far behind.

They stopped on reaching the house.

Strange! The front door was open!

"Who forgot to lock the door?" asked Florek, dashing inside. Before mother could reply, Florek had opened the door to the living room.

There by the Christmas tree, looking very much like Florek, stood Tatus!

When grandmother Godyslawa arrived, she, without

12. Lit-ter-gee.

a word, wrapped her arms around father, mother and son
— who were wrapped around each other.

We leave them there, just hugging each other . . .
What a Merry Christmas!

Ancile's Violin

Hannah knew in her heart that it wouldn't be a white Christmas. As she stood listlessly gazing out of the window of Mary's Diner (the only restaurant open on Christmas Eve), where she worked, she reflected how "tough" the times were. Her hazel eyes were clouded with unhappiness, her fading blonde hair slightly disarrayed and her waitress uniform a bit frayed. She was sort of a symbol of the depression, the poverty that darkened the skies of America in the early 1930's.

She was still standing by the cold window pane, when a young man of about thirty entered the diner. As he took off his soft, gray hat (men wore hats in those days), one couldn't help noticing his well-shaped head with raven-black beard and well-groomed hair parted on the side. His eyes, too, were dark and piercing — but not with hardness or lack of concern. They seemed to

---

1. An-seel, from the Latin word ancilla (an-sill-ah) meaning girl-servant. Jesus' Mother said to the angel that she was God's girl-servant (Luke: 1/38).

penetrate your soul, as if searching out the good in you.

"His eyes are like electric" mused Hannah as she set a cup and saucer before him. "A new pencil-striped suit. He must be some successful business man."

Politeness dictated that she greet all customers and engage them in friendly conversation before taking their orders. "Will you be able to make it home for Christmas?" she began. The diner's face saddened a little as he replied, "No, not this time, not for a month."

"What about you?" he added with interest.

Hannah's unhappiness welled over. The customer seemed to care. Words poured out of her and the man listened intently. Most customers like to talk about themslves and their problems, while the waitress patiently listens. Not this person. He leaned forward to catch every word. Hannah told him of her beloved daughter, Ancile, who had a great talent for the violin, even though she was only 12.

"She plays beautifully!She was born to the bow. Her teacher sees in her a budding genius. I've spent a small fortune from my meager salary (with tips, of course) to pay for her lessons. Ever since she was seven, she's been captivated by the strings and the melody they produce on that truly unique instrument, the violin." Then she sobbed softly, wiping her eyes with a pink kleenex, "Her teachers tell me she has outgrown her beginner's violin. She needs a full-sized one now. She's grown so. Her fingers are long, slender, deft, created to flick back and forth on the four strings that characterize this musical instrument."

The attentive listeners interrupted Hannah. "Are you unable to buy your Ancile a new violin?"

Hannah nodded sadly and reached for another tissue to wipe away her tears. "I was hoping to give her a new one for Christmas but it's impossible. Even a used one is out of the question. Musicians are always looking for a second-hand instrument themselves. I only have forty dollar saved. It would take at least another sixty."

A blast of cold air whistled into the restaurant as the door opened. Who would walk in but Ancile herself, violin case in hand. "Mother," she smiled, "I've finished my lessons for today. The teacher sent me home early because it's Christmas Eve.

Mother and daughter looked so alike. You could compare at once the similarities of face and features as well as contrast the work-worn 30-year old parent with the young, fresh 12 year old daughter. Customers looked up with approval at the pair. The quiet diner, too, cast appreciative glances at them with attentive gaze.

"Why not play for us?" he said, the moment they were introduced. "It's Christmas Eve; everyone is in mellow mood and soon will be going home. The boss won't mind, even if he hears about it!" Heads everywhere nodded in agreement, as all heard the conversation, the room being rather small.

To Ancile's questioning look, Hannah shrugged her shoulders, threw up her hands and happily announced, "Why not, it's Christmas Eve."

Gently, lovingly, Ancile removed her precious but out-grown stringed instrument from its worn, rather cheap, leatherette case, reached for the much used, slender bow, adjusted the violin under her thin yet shapely chin and began to play.

Not a coffee cup banged on its uneven saucer, not a fork or spoon rattled on its counter, no door slammed. Everyone stopped eating, drinking, conversing.

Sweet strains swept over the unexpected assembly. The magical moment was all Ancile's, as carol after carol enraptured the ear while Christmas peace and cheer suffused the heart.

"A rare artist, indeed" concluded the impressed stranger. Customers clapped and congratulated the young miss of only 12. Mother Hannah beamed — but, as customers began filing out,she returned to the stern world of reality. "We're closing now" she reminded the two talking to each other. "I still have a lot of work to do tonight. We'll have a quiet celebration tomorrow. Run along, dear Ancile. The cash register has to be checked and the receipts totaled. I'll be home in an hour." The girl hurried to please and accommodate her mom. She was soon gone, like a ray of spring sunshine amid winter's gloom.

The bearded stranger had been putting on his coat slowly, deep in thought. He pulled down the brim of his grey fedora hat, as men did in those days, and turning to Hannah remarked casually, "I have a violin that has been gathering dust for years in my closet. I really don't need it. I don't play. It belonged to my brother, who's long gone. I tell you what. I'll sell it to you for, say, forty dollars."

Hannah's hands, wiping a table, stopped suddenly still. They trembled there, in that eating place, that lonely fast-food kind of restaurant, the only one open on Christmas Eve.

"You mean it?" Hannah's voice quavered. "You're not putting me on?"

"I mean it," quietly retorted the man. "It would be just the kind of gift your" he emphasized, "that your daughter deserves."

Hannah already had her purse open. She fumbled for a hidden compartment, a fold within the purse, where she had "stashed" three ten dollar bills and two fives. He gestured, "No, not now, I'll bring the violin in the morning. Never pay for anything unless you see it."

That night Hannah tossed and turned in bed, pinching herself to make sure she wasn't dreaming. She thanked God for the unexpected, surprise Christmas present — and prayed fervently the man would return with it in the morning. Because she couldn't sleep, she was up early, tip-toeing out of the apartment so as not to disturb the deep sleep of Ancile. The stranger wasn't long in coming. Hannah gave a quick look at the violin, without taking it out of its ancient but well-preserved, leather, genuine leather, case, peeled off the bills in payment, dared to give the donor a bear-hug for being a Santa Claus and saw him leave with a quiet smile and a faint shadow of a bow.

What shouts of surprise! What shrieks of joy when Ancile spied the violin under the Christmas tree! She fondled it, pressed it to her bosom, stroked it, played it all day long. Strains of "Adeste Fideles," "Silent Night," and so many other ancient and mod carols filled the home — as they did in the restaurant the night before. It was as if Christmas had come to Hannah's home and an angel in human form was performing for the newly-born Baby of Bethlehem, the Christ-Child.

The next day was free, but the following day Ancile trudged through streets already powdered heavily with snow. Her heart sang in the spirit of the season with "Thank you, Jesus" for the God-given gift she received — from a man!

Her teacher in surprise stared at the violin as Ancile proudly displayed it. He examined it closely with unbelieving eyes, brought it under his sagging chin and began to play as Ancile wondered what all this meant.

"Unbelievable!" the teacher muttered after hearing the melodious tones rising from the stroked strings. "It, it must be a Stradivarius! Why it is, child! Look at these small letters on the edge!" Sure enough, Ancile could see the name "Stradivarius"[2] delicately carved into the specially treated, white, birch side of the violin.

"What does Strad, Stradi, Stradivarius mean, Mr. Mahan?" inquired Ancile, stumbling over the long word.

"My dear," breathing hard with emotion and excitement, replied the teacher, "I think I'm holding thousands of dollars in my hands. Oh my!" Gingerly, awed and extremely impressed, he laid the expensive, antique instrument on the piano near him. He went on to explain with many "O, dear" and "Oh, my," "Ancile, dear!" that a Stradivarius was a very expensive violin made by a master craftsman, Antonio Stradivari, who lived over 300 years ago in Italy. His violins became world-famous for their rich, resonant strings and beauty of construction. Specially treated wood, like split spruce, maple and birch, were used.

In other words, dear reader, Ancile received a treasure, an ancient, costly heirloom.

Was that quiet stranger, who sold for forty dollars what easily was worth forty thousand dollars, really a man?

It could have been God — in human form . . .

Ancile thought so, as she played on and on, becoming a world-famous violinist when she grew up.

Never a day passed, however, that she didn't thank God for His Christmas present to her that snowy day.

---

2. Strad-dyh-various.

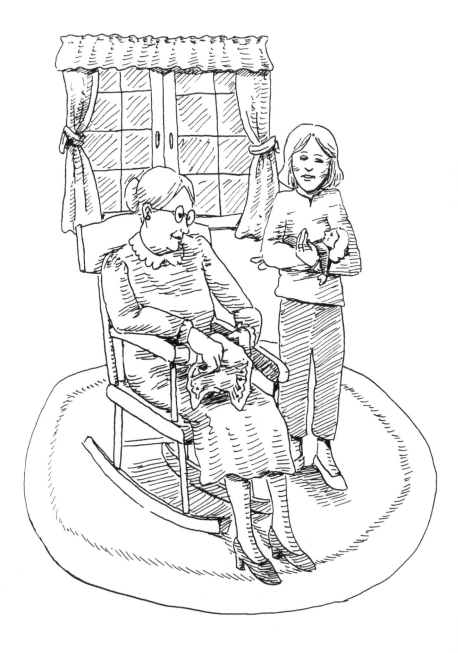

The Christmas Doll

Christmas vacation started early that year. I was too excited to remain calm. I had the "season's spirit bad," as dad said. So mother sent me off to grandma's. Staying with grandma at the time was my Aunt Lou. Hence, mother felt there were plenty of people, well, two, to entertain me where grandma lived. Mother needed to be alone to plan the family Christmas. I was too much for her.

At grandma's, Christmas preparations were also in full swing. Nothing escaped my notice. Everything piqued[1] my curiosity. What fascinated me most, however, was a darling little doll with the most adorable blue eyes. I was sure it was for me. When I questioned Aunt Lou, who sat sewing lovely, light-colored dresses for the doll, to my great disappointment Aunt Lou revealed to me that the doll was meant for Diane Drake, who was a daughter of one of Aunt Lou's friends.

It was to be a secret, Aunt Lou confided in me, but since she had spilled the beans, "Would you share the secret with me, not tell a soul and help me with the doll?" What could I say? I tried not to let tears flow as I wanted the doll so much for myself. I swallowed hard, nodded my

---

1. Pronounced, believe it or not, "peeked." It's a French word, meaning to stir up, arouse.

head, sniffled and quickly reached for a tissue as if to wipe my nose. I tried to keep back tears. I was pleased, however, that Aunt Lou confided[2] in me so much. She discussed every detail about the dresses that were sewn. She asked me what kind of bed would be best for the doll. Her kind eyes smiled beneath her white snowy hair as she consulted[3] me about the make of the mattress and type of pillows the doll's bed should have.

Sometimes, I did cry when alone, especially at night, reflecting that I was helping another girl, a total stranger to me, to be happy — while I was miserable. But to be a Christian, mother and dad often reminded me, you were to go through life spreading sunshine by doing "nice things" for others. I concluded sadly I had better consider my doing a nice thing for a girl I never saw or knew as a Christmas present from me to her "And out of love for You, dear Infant Jesus" I prayed piously.[4]

It was easier, then, to proceed with making dainty doll blankets that looked like miniature[5] baby blankets. When, however, Aunt Lou once asked, "How would Diane like her doll's hair-do to be?" I cringed[6] and almost cried out loud. I composed myself, that is, I smiled instead and forced myself to explain to Aunt Lou my idea of the doll's hair-styling. "What a pretty coiffure!"[7] Aunt Lou exclaimed. "You have good taste, child." I gathered from this, "coiffure" meant hair style. I was pleased both that my kindly aunt liked my suggestion and that I learned a

2. To confide in someone means to share personal thoughts and secrets with another trusted person.
3. To seek advice on something.
4. To pray with devotion and mean what you say.
5. Small-sized.
6. To shrink back, draw back.
7. Kwah-fyoor. It's a French word commonly used by hair stylists.

new word. I think we should learn as many words as we can every day. Grandma and Aunt Lou were always using words I never heard before but they always explained them to me when I asked.

Still, I wished the doll with my hair-style was mine and sighed wistfully, fighting off resentment[8] and renewing my resolution[9] to be a "good sport" and offer my share of the doll's creation to the Baby whose Birthday we would celebrate — as would Diane, no doubt. I sniffled anew and another tissue was drying my nose and a second one my eyes. Aunt Lou had left the room for a moment, so I afforded myself the luxury of a few more secret tears. "It's not easy to be good to others" I told myself once more in self-pity.

By now, it was only two days till Christmas. The doll and bed were nearly finished and I was to return home. "What a cute little outfit you made for that darling doll" grandma remarked, her gray, old eyes dancing with delight. I was flattered by the compliment[10] as grandma said goodbye to me. Aunt Lou gushed her thanks too, promising me a "nice" Christmas present for "being such a good, helpful girl — and so understanding of what Diane Drake would like her doll to be!"

I fled to the waiting car, failing this time to hide my hot tears flowing over my flushed face and burning cheeks. Grandma and Aunt Lou mistook my plight as sorrow that I had to leave them. This was true — but the tears were first and foremost a saying good-bye to a doll that would forever be to me only a dream.

Mother was unsympathetic when I let it slip that I felt

8. Sense of jealousy.
9. Strong intention.
10. Praise.

bad about Diane getting a doll I had helped create.
Mother simply stated, "Be glad you could do something
for others. Did you tell Jesus you were doing this out of
love for Him?" I nodded silently and slowly went to my
room. No one really understood how much I had come to
love that little doll. I even gave her a secret name, "Bonnie
Blue Eyes."

Finally, Christmas Eve arrived. No snow had fallen
all week but toward three o'clock in the afternoon, a few
flakes fluttered out of the sullen, overcast sky. The fading
light of what was one of the shortest days of the year
began to reveal a real, winter wonderland. By 7 o'clock
the snow stopped. The murky[11] clouds were scattered,
surrendering to a magnificent spangled, magic night. A
cold, crisp, silver, metallic moon shone like a newly
minted[12] dime in the dome of the star-lit sky.

Indoors, mother and dad invited us children, as
always, to help with decorating the Christmas tree. They
had already purchased our presents and hid them where
they thought we wouldn't find them till Christmas
morning. We knew where — but we never told them or
peeked or tried to open them. It was such a surprise to
open them with the whole family present, when we
gathered by the tree on Christmas Day, early. I consoled[13]
myself, somewhat, with the thought that I might get
something that would take my mind off my beloved
"Bonnie Blue Eyes."

But I dreamed about her all night long, caressing
her, embracing her, stroking her hair, the hair I styled
myself . . . The feather-tick, under which many people

11. Mur-key, meaning gloomy.
12. Freshly-coined or made.
13. Comforted.

slept in those days, because there was no heat during the night in the house, felt so snug and warm. Yet I felt it was "Bonnie" that made me feel the warmth most.

Morning was a moving, highly emotional[14] time as we children scampered out of bed, threw on our clothes or just flung a bathrobe over our pajamas and flew downstairs to our resplendent Christmas tree. It was always about 6 a.m., so outside it was still night, that glorious night of Jesus' Birth.

Excitement! Shouting and shrieks of delight as we tore open our presents — except this year I did not shriek or shout but gloomily untied the ribbons and unfolded the colorful Christmas wrappings carefully (for future use). Indifferently, I undid the red string that held the lid of the box securely in place, brushed the tissue paper aside as the lid fell to the floor.

"Could it be?"

"No it couldn't!"

"Impossible!"

"Yes it is!"

"IT'S BONNIE BLUE EYES!"

"MY DOLL!"

It was my turn to shout and scream with joy.

Then, I stared at the smiling faces of my family. They knew all along — and never told me! Dad winked at me. Mother made a gesture with her hands. I was in her arms in a flash, hugging and kissing her.

"Wait, wait!" mother counseled.[15] "Save this for the one who thought up the whole idea!"

A door opened upstairs, the door of the guest room that was seldom occupied. Down came, hair in curlers,

14. Full of feeling.
15. Advised.

cold cream on her face; a gorgeous robe, however, over her woolen night gown, yes, down came — Aunt Lou!

"Surprise! Surprise!" mother, dad and aunt cried to us — and especially to me.

Now it was Aunt Lou's turn to be fussed over by us children, who didn't know she arrived late last night, when we were asleep.

"Now" she asked gently, with her beautiful hands, those deft,[16] delicate hands reaching out to me, "Aren't you glad you helped make — 'Diane's' doll?"

How grateful I was for not being a "stinker" and helping Aunt Lou.

I was also grateful to Jesus. He must have smiled seeing me rocking "Bonnie Blue Eyes" in my arms.

16. Skillful.

82